If You Squint
At a Rhinoceros...

by Cynthia Tompkins Dunn

Illustrated by Stella M. Lopez

HARBINGER HOUSE
Tucson • New York

To our mothers

HARBINGER HOUSE, INC.
Tucson, Arizona

Copyright © 1990 by Cynthia Tompkins Dunn
Illustrations copyright © 1990 by Stella M. Lopez

Printed in Hong Kong.

Designed by Nancy J. Parker

Library of Congress Cataloging-in-Publication Data
Dunn, Cynthia Tompkins, 1955–
    If you squint at a rhinoceros / by Cynthia Tompkins Dunn;
illustrations by Stella M. Lopez.
        p.   cm.
    Summary: Fanciful verse and detailed illustrations present
information about dinosaurs.
    ISBN 0-943173-67-1
    1. Dinosaurs—Juvenile poetry. 2. Children's poetry, American.
[1. Dinosaurs—Poetry. 2. American poetry.] I. Lopez, Stella M.,
1955–, ill. II. Title.
PS3554.U4697813   1990
811 ' .54—dc20   90-30384

If You Squint At A Rhinoceros

If you squint at a rhinoceros,
You might see a triceratops there,
Or a flock of flying pelicans
Could look like pterodactyls in the air.

You can study fossils of dinosaur teeth,
Build skeletons from the bones found beneath,
And learn quite a lot about long ago,
But still there's so much you can't possibly know.

For instance, the dinosaurs, what colors were they?
Lavender, turquoise, or plain charcoal gray?
Close your eyes, let your thoughts run wild and free . . .
What colors are the dinosaurs that you see?

Don't be surprised when you open your eyes
At the dinosaurs that you find.
Do you really think we can call them extinct
When they live in our hearts and our minds?

Stegosaurus was as big as an elephant,
With a brain the size of a golf ball.
It's hard to believe that a creature so large
Had a brain so incredibly small.

Oh, he was a handsome fellow,
Who survived mostly on his looks.
Lucky for him that he lived long ago,
For I doubt he could've learned to read books.

While scientists speculate about the plates
That grew down his back in pairs,
I like to pretend something really absurd,
Like he kept his spare brains back there.

Stegosaurus

steg-o-SAWR-us

roofed lizard

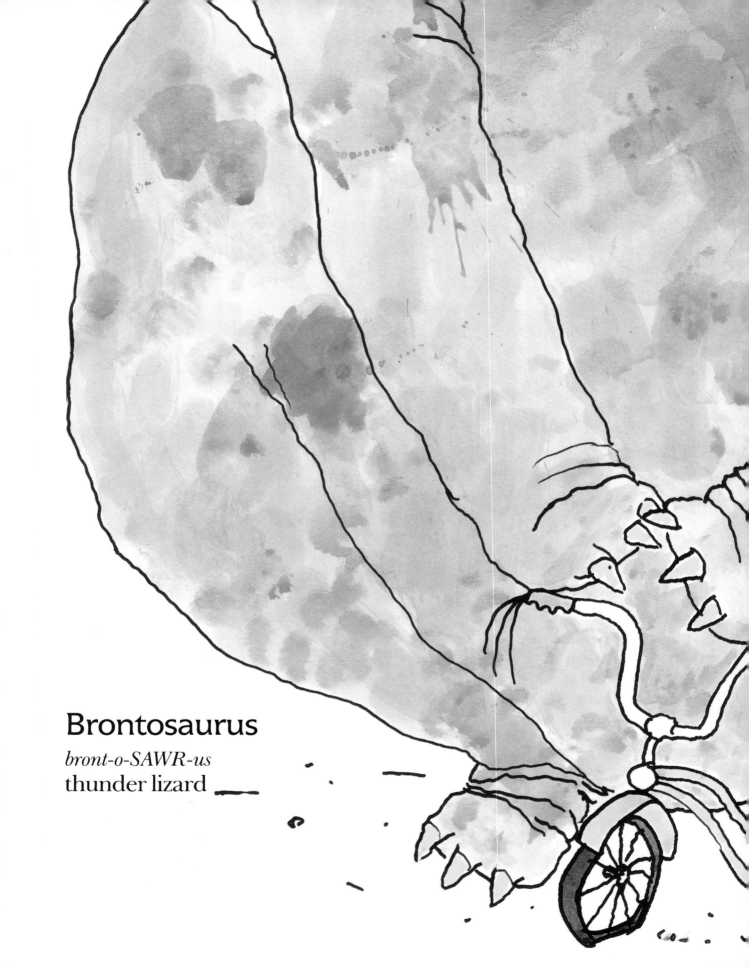

Brontosaurus

bront-o-SAWR-us
thunder lizard

Brontosaurus, it is said,
Had a brain in his tail
As well as his head.
Believe it or not,
For we'll never know,
But we know his tail followed
Where his head chose to go.

Thunder Lizard's legs
Were huge and pillar-like.
Wouldn't he look funny
If he chose to ride your bike?

Oviraptor

ov-ih-RAPT-or
egg thief

Eggs, Eggs,
Poached or fried,
Scrambled eggs,
True and tried.
Eggs over easy,
Pickled, or shirred,
Eggs are what
Oviraptor preferred.
Eggs Benedict,
Quiche or souffle,
Every style,
Every day.

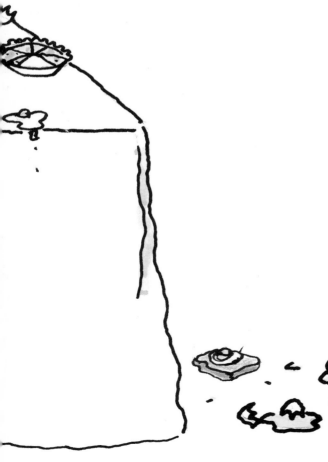

Triceratops

try-SER-a-tops
three-horned face

Never kiss a triceratops
Or you'll get a surprise,
He has a horn upon his nose
And two above his eyes!

Of course, that's not a problem,
Since you'll probably never see one,
But just in case you ever do,
I warn you—kissing one's not fun!

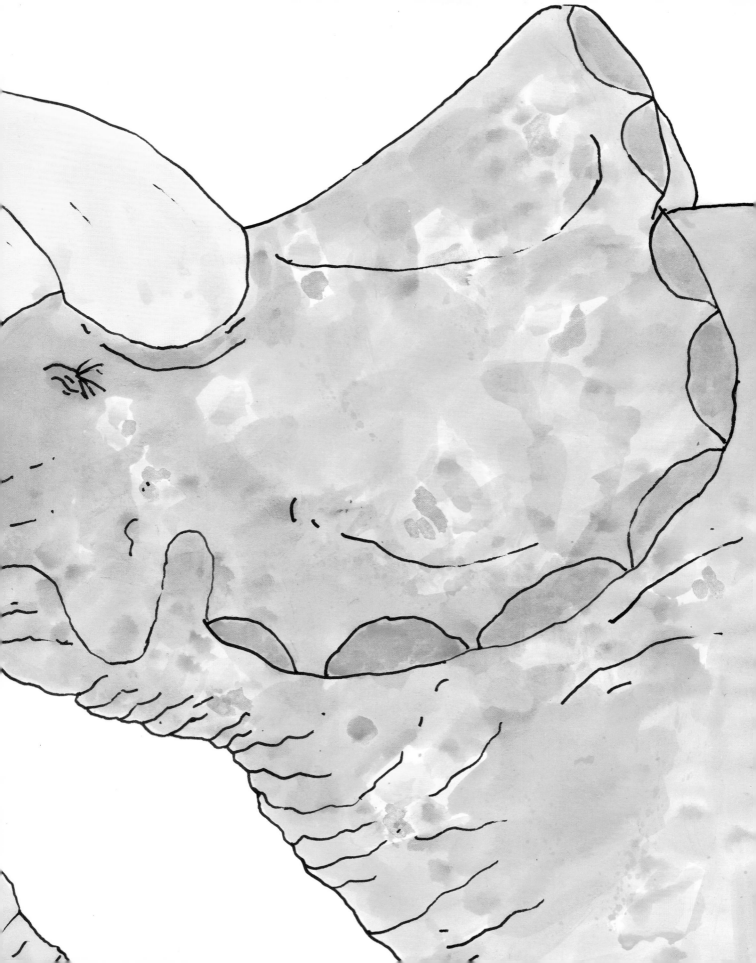

Chasmosaurus

KAZ-mo-sawr-us
ravine lizard

A young Chasmosaurus named Chad
Was feeling embarrassed and sad,
For he hadn't a frill
Like his big brother Bill
Or his dad and his grandfather had.

Young Chad asked big brother Bill
Why he alone had no frill.
Said Bill with a smile,
"Just wait a while,
And when you grow up you will!"

Deinonychus

dine-ON-ik-us
terrible claw

Dine on, dine on, Deinonychus,
I won't get in your way.
Your manners are just terrible
And you haven't much to say.

Rhamphorhynchus would have been
A dinosaur dentist's delight.
Just remind him to brush
Morning and night,
Teach him to floss
Till he gets it right,
And recommend braces
For his overbite.
And there's no need
To raise the chair—
He could have his teeth
Checked in midair,
And get them cleaned
While he's still there.
But, on second thought,
Who would dare?

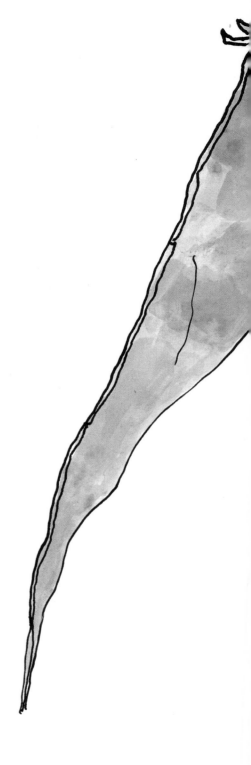

Rhamphorhynchus

ram-fo-RINK-us
narrow beak

Allosaurus likes to eat,
And eat and eat and eat,
But if you offered her a salad,
She'd say, "No, thanks, I just eat meat."

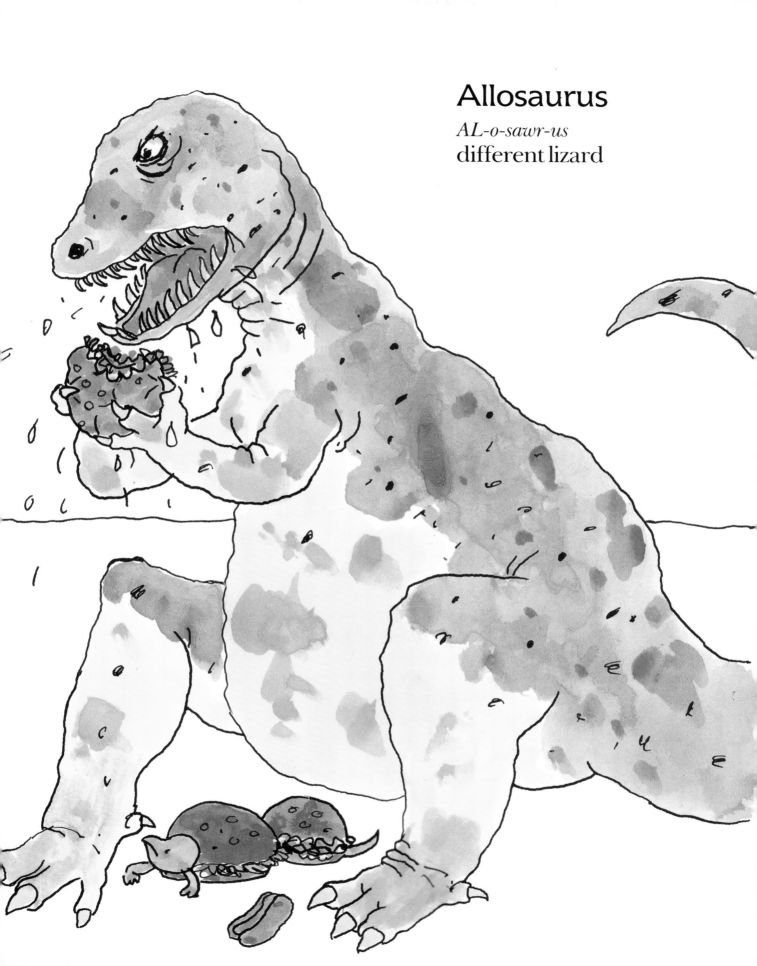

Allosaurus

AL-o-sawr-us
different lizard

I found myself a-wishing
On a sunny Saturday
That I could go a-fishing
The Elasmosaurus way.

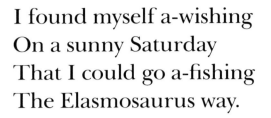

If my neck were longer,
Say twenty-five more feet,
And my teeth were sharper,
I could catch some fish to eat.

Of course, I'd be a lot too big
For swimming in a brook,
But it would solve my biggest problem . . .
I hate putting worms on hooks!

Elasmosaurus

ee-LAZ-mo-sawr-us
plated lizard

Gallimimus

gal-ih-MIME-us
hen mimic

Taller than a man,
She had skinny, bird-like legs.
Gallimimus kept her figure,
Eating mostly fruit and eggs.

She could have played piano
With her fingers and her toes,
But if her voice was beautiful,
No one really knows.

Nodosaurus had no teeth
And so he had no toothbrush.
Think of it!
The time he saved
By having none to wash.

Nodosaurus

NO-doh-sawr-us
lumpy lizard

The eggs in our refrigerator
Looked a little old,
Perhaps they'd kept so well preserved
By staying extra cold.
But when I told my mother
What I really felt was true,
"They look like Tyrannosaurus eggs,
Don't they look like them to you?"

Tyrannosaurus

ty-ran-o-SAWR-us
king lizard

She said she had no time
For silliness and jokes,
But when she cracked them open,
They had Tyrannosaurus yolks!
"See there!" I cried excitedly,
While cracking several more,
But poor Mother couldn't hear me,
She had fainted on the floor.

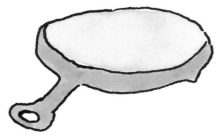

Mary made a Lambeosaurus
Out of white bread dough,
And every time she looked at it,
It seemed to grow and grow.

Its tail grew extra long,
Huge claws grew from its toes,
Its head grew up in a hatchet-shaped bump
And out in a duck-shaped nose.

Mary baked it in the oven
To take to school one day,
And for her science project
Mary got an A.

Lambeosaurus

LAM-be-o-sawr-us
Lambe's lizard

Edmontonia

ed-mun-TONE-ee-ah
found in Edmonton, Canada

My best friend is a dinosaur.
Her name is Edmontonia.
I love to sing and dance with her,
But she tramples my mother's begonias.

Edmontonia is a magical creature,
A whimsical, witty surprise.
She likes to play tricks on my brother,
But I get blamed when he cries.

She's really a wonderful friend to have,
Honestly one of a kind,
And if my family can't see her,
It's because she lives in my mind.

Cynthia Dunn and Stella Lopez have been friends since child-
hood. Now their children are friends.

Stella runs a bookstore and Cynthia has an art gallery. Once a
week they meet to work together—they trade stories, share ideas,
and laugh a lot. Cynthia has been writing poems since third
grade. Stella has been drawing and painting for longer than
she can remember.

If You Squint at a Rhinoceros . . . is their first book but they have
ideas for a lot more.